Metu Neter

Graphic Novel Manuscript
Book 1

By Ausar Kauba

AUSAR KAUBA

All Rights Reserved

Copyright © 2023 by Ausar Kauba

No part of this book may be reproduced or transmitted, downloaded, distributed, reverse engineered, or stored in or introduced into any information storage and retrieval system, in any form or by any means, including photocopying and recording, whether electronic or mechanical, now known or hereinafter invented without permission in writing from the publisher.

Dorrance Publishing Co
585 Alpha Drive
Suite 103
Pittsburgh, PA 15238
Visit our website at www.dorrancebookstore.com

ISBN: 979-8-88925-432-4
eISBN: 979-8-88925-932-9

CHAPTER 1
A Gift From The Gods

Act 1:

The city of New York is bustling with life, but few know what lies beneath the hustle and bustle. Shepsu Aba King, a young man from NYC, a pacifist by nature, lives an ordinary life. But he is about to discover that his life is anything but ordinary. On his 14th birthday, he wakes early, 6:15 a.m., from the same recurring nightmare of an evil figure in an Egyptian tomb killing the King. He brushes this dream off as just another dramatic moment in his mediocre life, gets dressed, and heads out to the bus stop for school. While waiting for the bus, he's approached by his bullies, and one of them slaps Shepsu on the head. A group of three kids, Kai, Lamar, and Jamal, that call themselves the Misfitz. Kai Malcolm, the leader of the group, looks down on Shepsu because he is against violence and fighting. Kai looks at this as weakness and cowardly behavior. While Shepsu may not fight, he's not afraid to speak up and defend himself through words and sarcasm.

KAI: "That looked like it hurt, Shitsu. You got my lunch money, nerd!" SHEPSU: "Dang, you broke again already? Don't you come from money too? How tragic."
Kai punches Shepsu in the face: "SMARTASS!" and the Misfitz' begin beating on Shepsu as he lays there in the fetal position. Just then Shepsu's best friend, Skylar Akira, shows up to help.

SKYLAR: "HEY, BUTT MUNCHERS! LEAVE 'EM ALONE!"

LAMAR: "Or what? You'll throw a book at us? He laughs.

JAMAL: "WOOOW, he needs a girl to save him! What a joke! Hahaha."

Skylar smirks and pushes her glasses up in classic anime fashion. Then she grabs a book that looks to be Game of Thrones and flings it right at Jamal's head. Blood splats from his forehead in a comical manner shocking Lamar.

LAMAR: "Holy shit! She did it!"

SKYLAR screams: "BE CAREFUL WHAT YOU ASK FOR! NOW BEAT IT!"

Kai spits on the ground in an expression of disrespect to Skylar and Shepsu. He then rallies the Misfitz, and as he leaves, he turns to Shepsu,

KAI: "This isn't over, Nerd. She won't be there every time."
Shepsu wipes his bruised chin and responds confidently: "Whatever, Meathead."

The Misfitz take their leave and fade into the horizon.

SKYLAR: UGH! It's too early for those DIRTBAGS!"

SHEPSU: "I appreciate you, though. Don't sweat it."

SKYLAR: "How are you? They didn't hurt you, did they?"

SHEPSU: "Nah. Of course not. Kai's right is always predictable. Oh yeah, you can't forget this."

Shepsu picks up the book Skylar threw at Jamal.

SHEPSU: "Your weapon, M'lady. But you never had to throw a whole book at him."

He laughs.

SKYLAR: "Hey, a Lannister always pays their debts." A reference to Game of Thrones, the book that was thrown.

SKYLAR: "Let's get out of here. This isn't how you should start your birthday."

Skylar helps Shepsu up. He dusts himself off and they both leave heading back to Shepsu's house.

FADE OUT

Act 2:

INT. SHEPSU'S HOUSE

Shepsu and Skylar walk into the house shortly after the incident with the Misfitz, talking about anime, space, and time, quantum physics, and other nerdy things they enjoy together. The living room is filled with Egyptian and African decor. As they walk, they see Shepsu's grandmother sitting in her satin green recliner. Shepsu and Skylar call her Nana. She's a short and stout woman, maybe five feet tall. She has gray hair and wears a matching tribal hair scarf and dress with triangular glasses that occlude her eyes.

NANA: "I know I'm old, but school can't possibly be over already?" She gets up. "And what happened to my baby's face? Was it those rotten bebe kids again?" SHEPSU: "It's nothing, Nana. Classic Kai. I'm fine."
NANA: "What did I teach you? Violence is never the answer... but if someone puts their hands on you..."

Nana appears in a boxing ring and throws a powerful uppercut. NANA: "NANA SAID KNOCK YOU OUT!"

Shepsu goes into the kitchen and reaches for an apple in the fridge: "You also said, 'what's the point of evolution if we're gonna act like apes?'"
NANA: "I said that? That doesn't even sound like me."
SHEPSU: "Probably 'cause you had your hearing aid off again."

Shepsu and Nana have these kinds of back and forths all the time. It's a usual family squabble. Skylar intervenes and asks if they are going to go at each other every time they speak, and kisses Nana on the cheek. Nana thanks Skylar for helping Shepsu with those bullies and tells the kids that Shepsu has a birthday gift on the roof. Shepsu gets upset and is reluctant to accept it, because he's a believer in exchanging gifts and he didn't get her anything. Regardless, the two hop out the window and head up the fire escape to see the present.

NANA: "Be careful. The stars can tell you a lot about yourselves." "Maybe more than you want to know," she finishes suspensefully.

AUSAR KAUBA

As Shepsu and Skylar reach the roof, Shepsu's eyes flooded with tears and he screams with excitement. The gift is a Celestial Neutron 130 SLT Telescope designed by Sakura Co., the leading tech company around the world. Shepsu has wanted this telescope for years, but because they don't have much money, Shepsu would craft makeshift telescopes to gaze at the stars. Astronomy and astrophysics have been a passion of his since he was five years old after seeing a shooting star fly through the sky. Nana told him that these stars are gods soaring through the cosmos granting wishes to those who believe. Shepsu, being the kind hearted giver he is, wished for Skylar to win you Little League Softball championship, and when she did, Shepsu was sold that the stars are more than just beautiful, they are magic.

SKYLAR: "It's going to be hard to see through if you keep crying like that." Shepsu with a face full of tears: "I just love it so much! OMG it even has the 800MM Zoom! I can see every single star!"

Shepsu continues to enjoy his new gift while Skylar enjoys the summer morning breeze. As Shepsu looks on, he discovers Orion's Belt visible more than he's ever seen with his makeshift telescopes.

SHEPSU: "Sky come look!" You can still see Orion's Belt. That bright orange one, that's Betelguese... and right there, that's Orion's Belt, see?" He points.

SKYLAR: "I know, Shep. You're not the only one who likes astronomy here," she replies.

SHEPSU: "I know I know! I just get so excited about this stuff, y'know? Like, did you know that when the Egyptians built the Pyramids of Giza, each pyramid points to one of the stars in Orion's Belt? One day, I'll see the stars for myself! I have to know what's up there. The Egyptians were scholars beyond their time."

The two continue to look upon the stars and enjoy the morning air, not to mention the excitement of skipping school. Shepsu sees a blinding glare in the lens of the telescope. He squints and steps back to view it with his own eyes. The two stare in shock and awe as they see a gigantic fiery meteor hurtling through the atmosphere.

SHEPSU & SKYLAR: "OH... MY... GOD!"

CHAPTER 1 END

CHAPTER 2
I'm A Pharaoh?!

Act 1:

INT. ROOFTOP—DAY

Shepsu and Skylar were looking up at the night sky, admiring the stars, when they saw something coming down from the sky. It was blazing a path of light, and they knew it was a meteorite. The meteorite crashed in a nearby park.

SHEPSU: That was a legit meteor! I can't believe I just saw that!

SKYLAR: WOW! Wait a minute. I think that landed in J.R. Park. That's up the street! Come on!

SHEPSU: WHATCHU MEAN "COME ON?" Didn't you hear me?! That's a ME-TE-OR! I'm not tempting God today.

SKYLAR: So what, you gonna be a coward again?
SHEPSU: DON'T CALL ME A COWARD BULLET NOSE!

EXT. ROOFTOP

So Shepsu and Skylar decided to investigate. When they got to the park, they were astonished to find that the meteorite wasn't a meteor at all, but a woman. She was dressed in ancient clothes, and she had a mysterious look about her.

WOMAN: Wow! Not even a scratch! Probably could have done without the crash though. But it looks like Seker's Gaia Shield came in handy. Now let's start by searching for the Young Prince.

The woman starts to have a wave of emotions. First, she's excited, then depressed and hopeless, after that optimistic, and finally furious.

WOMAN (excited): YALLA! I MADE IT! I MADE IT! NEW MISSION! LET'S GET IT!

WOMAN (depressed): But what if the young prince is already DEAD?! I've failed you, Pharaoh! DARN IT ALL!

WOMAN (optimistic): NO! I mustn't think like that. Shai has spoken, Hator. This is his destiny. Happy thoughts!

WOMAN (furious): IF IT WEREN'T FOR THAT DAMN SET, WE WOULDN'T EVEN BE IN THIS MESS! YOU KNOW WHAT, FORGET THE PRINCE! I'M COMING FOR YOU SET! LET'S END THIS RIGHT NOW!

Skylar and Shepsu look down at her frantic behavior from atop the crater. They are astonished that the meteor turned out to be a woman, let alone a bipolar one. She looks up to see she's being watched and notices Shepsu instantly. WOMAN: HERU! I FOUND YOU!

SHEPSU: Hay-Who??

She jumps out of the crater at break-neck speed and tackles Shepsu, chest first. They fall to the ground and Skylar is at a loss for words.

WOMAN: I can't believe it's really you! MUNDHISH!
The woman gets up from landing on Shepsu, and Skylar, in a fit of jealous rage, grabs

Shepsu by the collar.

SKYLAR: GET IT TOGETHER, YOU LITTLE PERV!

The woman introduces herself as Hator, and she told them that she had been sent to the future, just as Shepsu had been, from ancient Egypt. Shepsu and Skylar were in disbelief, but Hator made it clear that she was telling the truth. She told them that she had been sent to help them in their mission, and that she would do whatever it took to make sure they succeeded. Just then, police arrive in response to the meteor crash. Shepsu and Skylar cannot afford to get caught up with the police about this, so they run off as Hator follows.

CHAPTER 2 END

Shepsu Aba King

Shepsu Aba King is a young man from Harlem, New York. He is an aspiring astrophysicist, and his dream is to one day explore the mysteries of the cosmos. He is an incredibly intelligent, hard-working, and determined individual. He's an introvert who loves spending time alone with his thoughts, exploring the night sky, and when he's not alone, he's spending time with his best friend, Skylar Akira. Cracking jokes, talking favorite tv shows, the cosmos, and humanities flaws and accomplishments.

Skylar Akira

Skylar Akira is a young lady with a passion for softball. She was a star player, and at the age of 15, she took her high school team to nationals. But after that, she mysteriously stopped playing and never spoke about it again. Her life changed drastically after her father passed away in an unexpected cave-in during a family trip. She's a quiet and introverted person who loves reading and stargazing with Shepsu. Despite her loss, she is determined to create a better furure for herself and those around her.

HATOR

Hator is the Goddess of love and compassion, and she is cartoonishly bipolar. Her emotions fluctuate at random moments, making her a different person to be around at times. Hator was sent to the "future" on a mission to train Shepsu for his destiny as the Pharaoh of Kemet. When she was a child, she lost her leg in a battle with a fierce God, but her mentor and friend, Osar, was able to use his power to restore it in crystall-ized ice. Although her emotions fluctuate, she is mostly a bubbly and energetic woman with a penchant forgetting into trouble.

Kai Malcolm

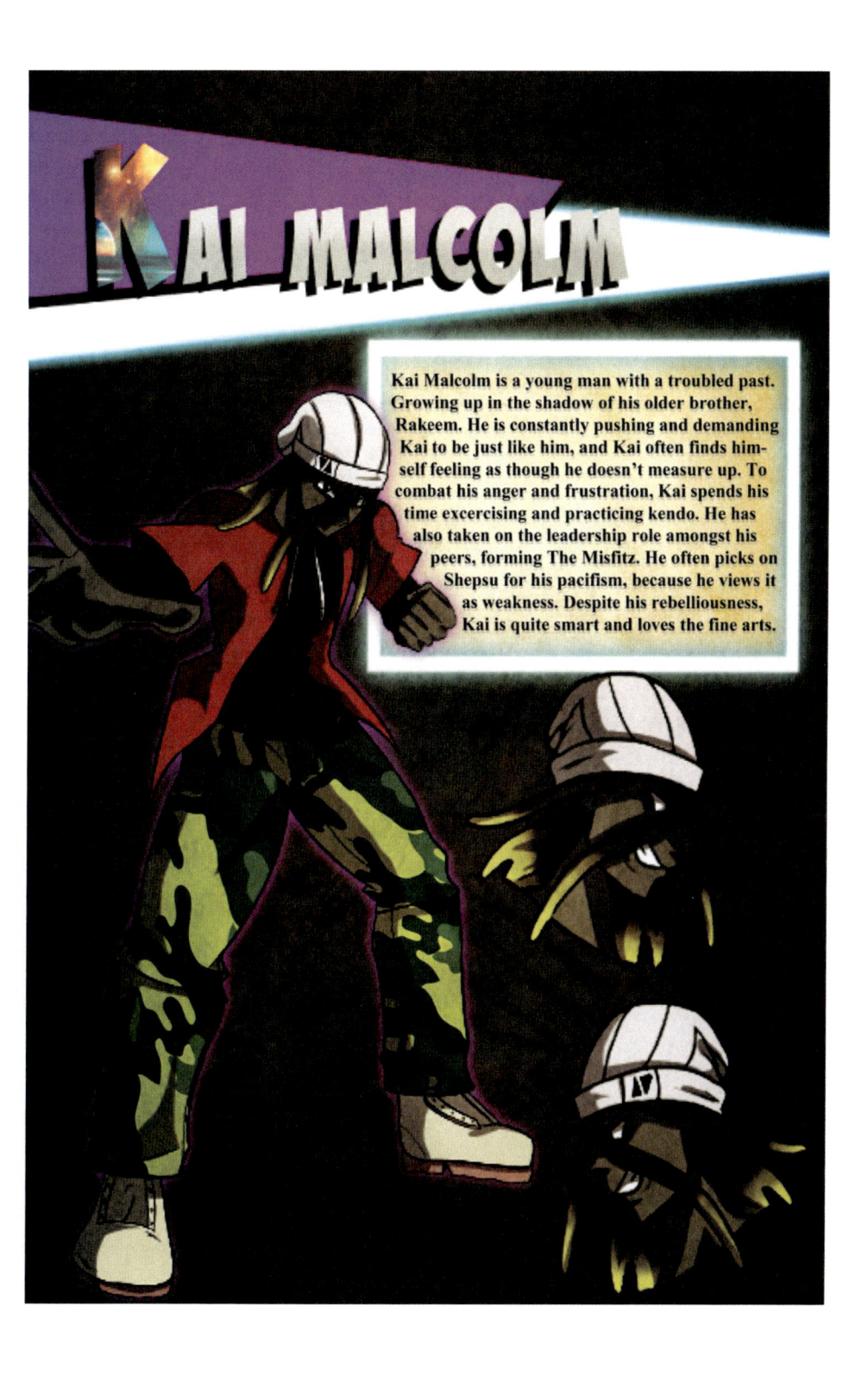

Kai Malcolm is a young man with a troubled past. Growing up in the shadow of his older brother, Rakeem. He is constantly pushing and demanding Kai to be just like him, and Kai often finds himself feeling as though he doesn't measure up. To combat his anger and frustration, Kai spends his time excercising and practicing kendo. He has also taken on the leadership role amongst his peers, forming The Misfitz. He often picks on Shepsu for his pacifism, because he views it as weakness. Despite his rebelliousness, Kai is quite smart and loves the fine arts.

JAMAL BROWN

Jamal is a young man living in a rough neiborhood. He is a member of the notorious gang, The Misfitz, alongside his best friend, Lamar, and his cousin Kai. Jamal is a troublemaker and a risk taker, often getting his friends into trouble. He grew up in a home with his single mother and young sister. With his father's absence, he found solace in the streets forming bonds with the wrong crowd. Jamal is quite skilled at engineering, and holds loyalty dear to his morales. He's not afraid to stand up for what he believes in and will do what it takes to make sure his gang is well respected.

LAMAR JOHNSON

Lamar is a young man from a nice neighborhood in Upper Manhattan. His father is a pastor and mother is a nurse, so his childhood isn't from a broken home. Despite this, his father was often too busy with the church, and his mother working long hours at the hospital, leaving Lamar to find his own way. So he found solace in Jamal and Kai and joined The MisFitz. Lamar is still struggling to find balance between his family's expectations and the loyalty to his brotherhood. Lamar is a gentle soul who loves helping others with a great sense of humor. He is a natural leader and often takes charge in situations.

NANA

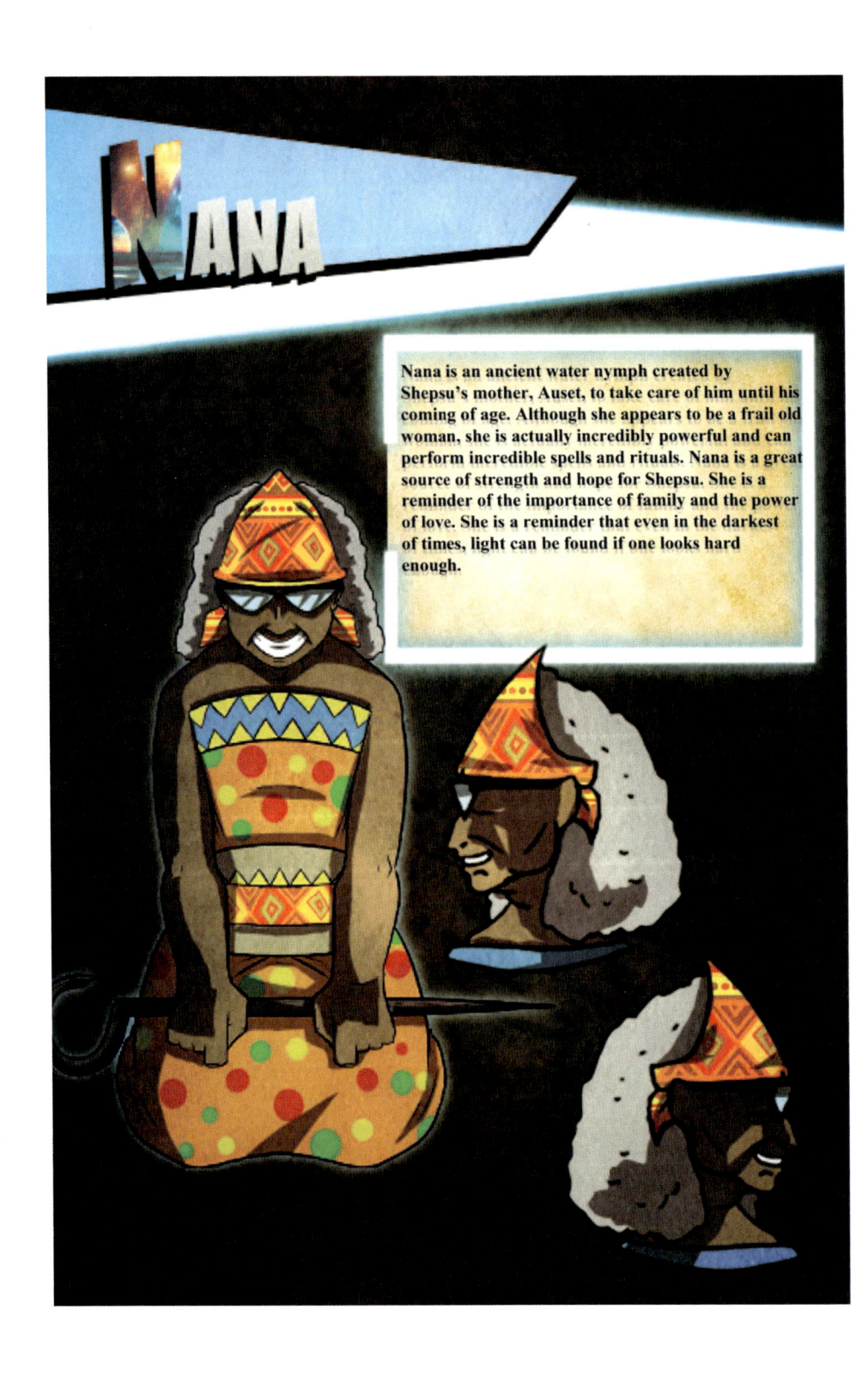

Nana is an ancient water nymph created by Shepsu's mother, Auset, to take care of him until his coming of age. Although she appears to be a frail old woman, she is actually incredibly powerful and can perform incredible spells and rituals. Nana is a great source of strength and hope for Shepsu. She is a reminder of the importance of family and the power of love. She is a reminder that even in the darkest of times, light can be found if one looks hard enough.

RAKEEM MALCOLM

Rakeem Malcolm is the CEO of the world's leading clothing brand, Drip Inc. Rakeem took over his father's company after he was assassinated during his own Gala. Rakeem quickly rose to prominence And success, becoming the face of the company and beloved by the public. His charisma and charm won over the hearts of the masses, but his true nature was hidden to the eyes of the public. He works in secret with a powerful group of world leaders to bring back the God of Chaos, Set, and take control of the new world they plan to create. He is determined to gain power, and no one will stand in his way

AGENT C

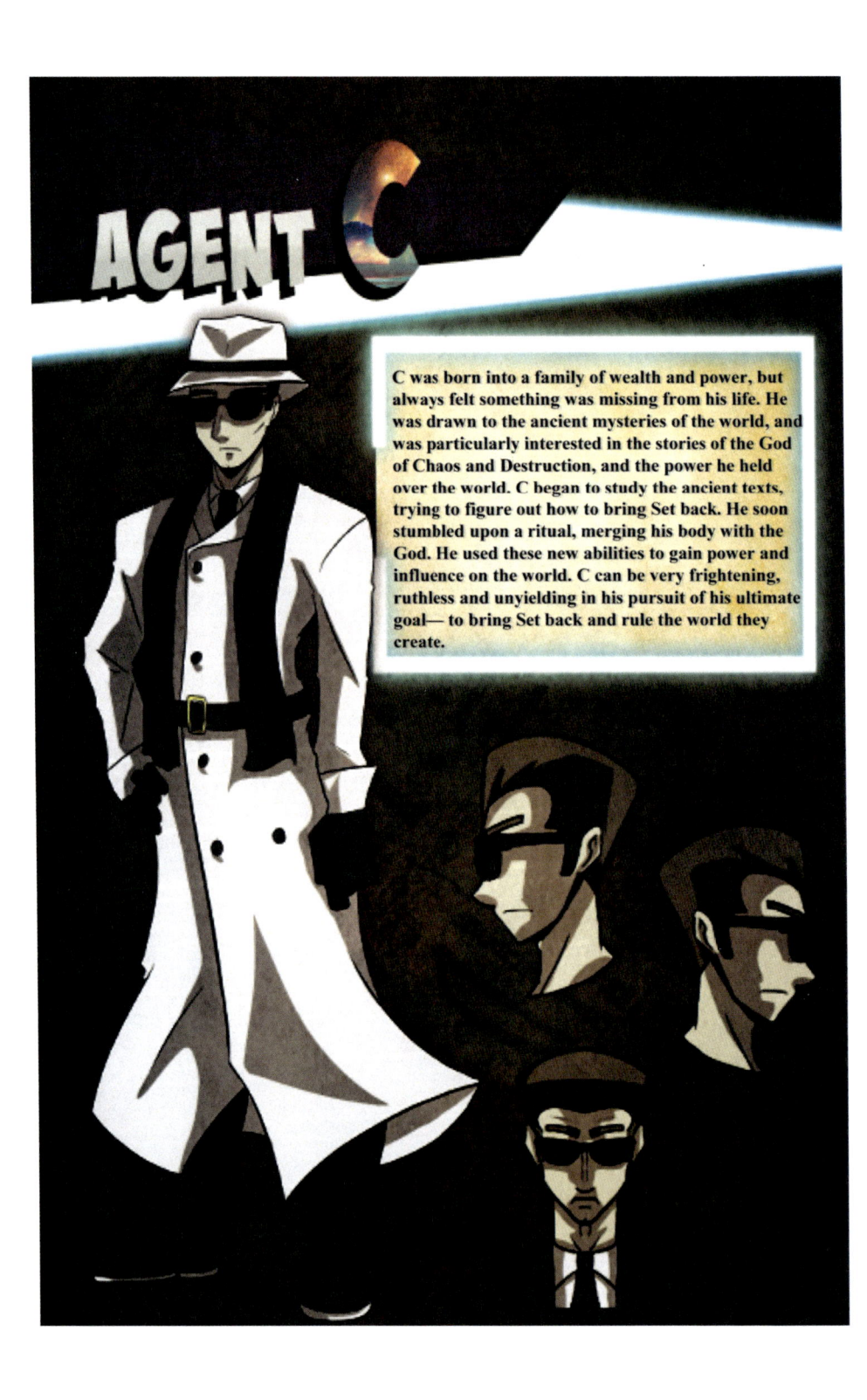

C was born into a family of wealth and power, but always felt something was missing from his life. He was drawn to the ancient mysteries of the world, and was particularly interested in the stories of the God of Chaos and Destruction, and the power he held over the world. C began to study the ancient texts, trying to figure out how to bring Set back. He soon stumbled upon a ritual, merging his body with the God. He used these new abilities to gain power and influence on the world. C can be very frightening, ruthless and unyielding in his pursuit of his ultimate goal— to bring Set back and rule the world they create.

AKI AKIRA

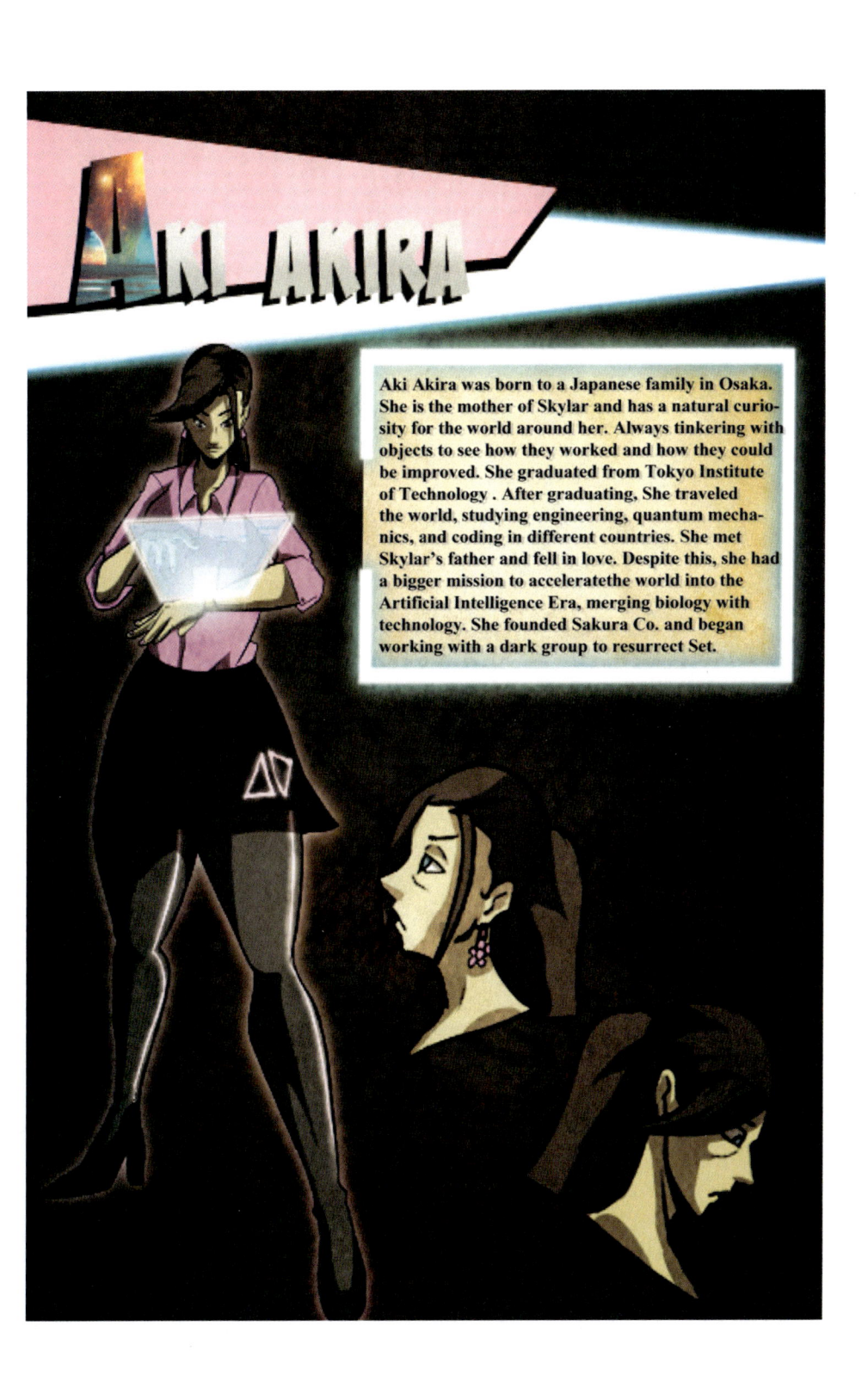

Aki Akira was born to a Japanese family in Osaka. She is the mother of Skylar and has a natural curiosity for the world around her. Always tinkering with objects to see how they worked and how they could be improved. She graduated from Tokyo Institute of Technology . After graduating, She traveled the world, studying engineering, quantum mechanics, and coding in different countries. She met Skylar's father and fell in love. Despite this, she had a bigger mission to acceleratethe world into the Artificial Intelligence Era, merging biology with technology. She founded Sakura Co. and began working with a dark group to resurrect Set.

AADEN DAROOD

Aaden Darood was born in Somalia, a small African nation plagued with war, famine, and poverty. Growing up in such a hostile environment have Aaden a deep understanding of the world, and a strong sense of justice. He's determined to make a difference and end his people's suffering. He was left alone after his parents death, and took to the seas where he became a pirate, raiding ships and taking whatever he could. He gained a crew and a strong reputation, seeking to liberate Somalia. He works in secret with a dark group of world leaders to bring about his vision.

VLADIMIR ROMANOV

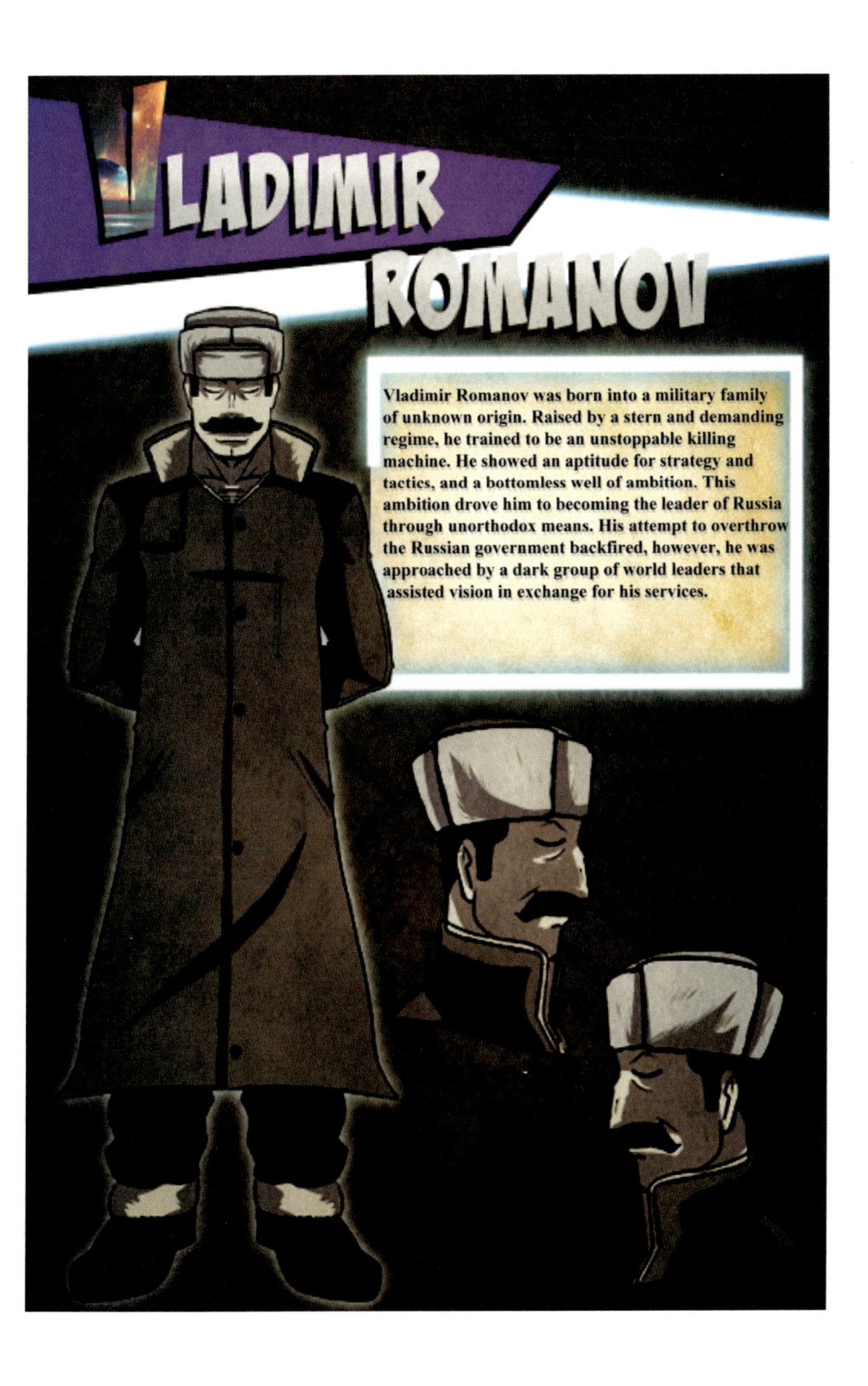

Vladimir Romanov was born into a military family of unknown origin. Raised by a stern and demanding regime, he trained to be an unstoppable killing machine. He showed an aptitude for strategy and tactics, and a bottomless well of ambition. This ambition drove him to becoming the leader of Russia through unorthodox means. His attempt to overthrow the Russian government backfired, however, he was approached by a dark group of world leaders that assisted vision in exchange for his services.

AUTHOR'S NOTE

Thank you for reading my book! It has been an honor to have you take a journey with me through this story. I hope that you enjoyed the characters, the plot, and the overall experience of reading my book. Your support, encouragement, and feedback throughout the writing process were invaluable and I am forever grateful. I am humbled and appreciative of the time you have taken to read my work. These characters are meant to be the representation of us all and finding the divine power inside ourselves that design who we are and what our purpose is. Shespu being a representation of Heru, or more commonly known by his Greek name, Horus. Heru is the 'child of prophecy,' if you will. He symbolizes the struggles for freedom within us all and it's where the term "hero" derives. A fitting name for a protagonist.

Leading into Book 2, we can begin to dive deeper into the plot direction, character development, relations, and backstories, expand on the world-building, and everything else this "Metu-verse" has to offer. Your support, encouragement, and kind words have been invaluable, and I am thankful for the chance to have been able to share my story with you. Thank you for being part of this journey and for reading my book.

Blessings,
Ausar Kauba

Made in the USA
Monee, IL
30 January 2025

3b3f17b9-62e1-450a-9216-b5b07f707badR01